THE KINGFISHER BOOK OF

NURSERY
TALES

For Jack and Conrad with much love – **V. F.**
To Tatum and Jim – **S. L.**

*A huge THANK YOU to Ann-Janine, Suzanne,
Miranda and Nia, our editors and designer.
They are all truly wonderful.*
– **V. F. & S. L.**

KINGFISHER
An imprint of Kingfisher Publications Plc
New Penderel House, 283-288 High Holborn
London WC1V 7HZ
www.kingfisherpub.com

First published in hardback by Kingfisher 2003
This edition published by Kingfisher 2004
2 4 6 8 10 9 7 5 3 1

Text copyright © Vivian French 2003
Illustrations copyright © Stephen Lambert 2003

A CIP catalogue record for this book is available from the British Library.

ISBN 0 7534 0991 7
1TR/0604/TWP/CG(CG)/150ENSOMA

Printed in Singapore

THE KINGFISHER BOOK OF
NURSERY
TALES

Retold by
VIVIAN FRENCH

Illustrated by
STEPHEN LAMBERT

KINGFISHER

CONTENTS

FOREWORD

I have always loved nursery tales. They're such fun, catching at every small child's imagination with their magical mix of talking animals, ridiculous adults, and inanimate objects that leap into life. There's more to these stories than just fun, however; they serve up their fantastical world with a good dollop of common sense, a warm and comforting reinforcement of family solidarity, and a simple but clear morality. Big Bad Wolves go hungry, but hard-working little pigs live happily ever after. It's a reassuring order of things for the very young, especially at bedtime. There may be a baddie or three out there, but keep to the rules and you'll be all right . . . And, besides, it's hugely enjoyable hearing a story about a naughty girl who eats somebody else's porridge and then gets chased by bears!

My youngest daughter always asked for "The Enormous Turnip" because she liked the little white mouse so much – he was only tiny, but he was still needed to heave that turnip out of the ground. In nursery tales even the smallest of all can save the day. She also loved "The Three Wishes" because, even though she felt that she wasn't as clever as her three big sisters, she was NEVER as silly as the woodcutter and his wife. She knew – as do all children who hear this story – EXACTLY what she'd do if she ever was given three wishes!

I have written these stories to be read aloud. Sharing a story this way is truly magical; my father read to me, I read to my daughters, and now my eldest daughter reads in her turn to my grandson, Jack. I love listening in and watching his face light up when he sees the pictures – and I just can't wait to show him Stephen Lambert's utterly glorious illustrations for these nursery tales. Stephen has done far far more than just illustrate the characters dancing and prancing through the pages; he has given each one a reality and life of their very own. He leaves me breathless with admiration. I've never seen a wolf with such style and panache as the one that visits Grandmother's house!

Finally, I have tried to allow for all styles of reader: those who favour the dramatic approach, and those who have a quieter style. There is no one right way to read these stories – whatever is right for you is right for those who listen. Your voice is the voice they love best . . . and I wish you many, many hours of very happy reading.

February 2003

THE THREE LITTLE PIGS

Once there was a pigsty, and in the pigsty lived an old mother pig and her three little piggywigs. At first they were happy, but each and every day the three little pigs grew bigger . . . and bigger . . . and bigger.

At last the day came when Mother Pig said, "Oink! There's no room at all in this sty! I'm squished and I'm squashed and I can't turn round!

It's high time, my piggywigs, for you to find your own houses. Off you go – but do be careful in the deep dark woods! Always watch for the big bad wolf!"

The three little pigs nodded. "Yes, dear mother," they said. "We will find our own houses, and when you come and visit we will have parsnips and peppercorns and green pea soup!"

So off went the three little pigs – pitter patter, pitter patter, pitter patter – into the deep dark woods.

They hadn't gone far when they met a man, and the man was carrying a bundle of hay.

"Oh, Mr Man," said the first little pig. "Please may I have some of your hay to make a house?"

"Well now, piggywig," said the man, "I don't see why not. Help yourself."

The first little pig took a heap of hay, and he built himself a neat little house.

"Here I am and here I stay,
Happy in my house of hay!"

he sang, and he kissed his brother and sister goodbye.

The second and the third little pigs went pattering on along the path.

They hadn't gone far when they met a man, and the man was carrying a bundle of sticks.

"Oh, Mr Man," said the second little pig. "Please may I have some of your sticks to make a house?"

"Some sticks, piggywig?" the man said. "Of course you may."

The second little pig took a pile of sticks, and he built himself a neat little house.

"Hay is grass and sticks are wood.
My house of sticks is very good!"
he sang, and he kissed his sister goodbye.

The third little pig went pattering along the path all on her own.

She hadn't gone far when she met a man, and the man was carrying a heavy hod of bricks.

"Oh, Mr Man," said the third little pig. "Please may I have some of your bricks to make a house?"

"Piggywig," said the man, "I would be glad to give you some bricks."

"Thank you, thank you!" said the third little pig, and she built herself a sweet little, neat little house.

"A house of hay, a house of sticks,
I'm happy in my house of bricks!"

she sang. She lit a fire, put a big pot of water on to boil, and began to cut up parsnips and peppercorns.

In the darkest part of the deep dark woods the big bad wolf yawned, sat up, and sniffed the air.

"I smell smoke!" he said to himself. "Now, who can be cooking in my deep dark woods?" And he began pad pad padding along the path.

He hadn't gone far when he saw the house of hay, and the first little pig happily sowing peppercorn seed. The big bad wolf's stomach began to rumble.

"I see DINNER!" he said.

He began pad pad padding nearer and nearer until – SNAP! He stepped on a twig.

"Oink!" said the first little pig. He ran inside his house and pulled the door shut.

The big bad wolf bent down to the keyhole, and smiled a big bad smile.

"Piggywig! Piggywig! Let me come in!" he called.

"No no! By the hairs on my chinny chin chin, I will NOT let you in!" shouted the first little pig.

"Then I'll huff, and I'll puff, and I'll BLOW your house down!" growled the wolf.

He took a deep breath, and he huffed, and he puffed, **and he huffed, and he puffed –**

and he blew the little
pig's hay house down –

SWOOSH!

"Oink! Oink! Oink!" squealed the first little pig, and he ran and he ran until he came to the house of sticks. The second little pig was outside, happily planting parsnips.

"It's the wolf! It's the wolf! It's the big bad wolf!" gasped the first little pig. He and his brother rushed inside and slammed the stick door shut.

The big bad wolf came panting after them. He smiled a bigger big bad smile.

"Piggywigs! Piggywigs! Let me come in!" he called.

"No no! By the hairs on our chinny chin chins, we will NOT let you in!" shouted the two little pigs.

"Then I'll huff, and I'll puff, and I'll BLOW your house down!" snarled the wolf.

He took a deep breath, and he huffed, and he puffed, **and he huffed, and he puffed –** and he blew the little pig's stick house down –

CRASH!

"Oink! Oink! Oink!" squealed the two little pigs, and they ran and they ran until they came to the house of bricks.

The third little pig was sitting on her doorstep podding peas.

"It's the wolf! It's the wolf! It's the big bad wolf!" gasped the two little pigs. The three of them raced inside, and the third little pig locked and bolted the door firmly shut.

The big bad wolf came puffing after them. He smiled his biggest big bad smile.

"Piggywigs! Piggywigs! Let me come in!" he called.

"No no! By the hairs on our chinny chin chins, we will NOT let you in!" shouted the three little pigs.

"Then I'll huff, and I'll puff, and I'll BLOW your house down!" roared the wolf.

He took a deep breath, and he huffed, and he puffed, and he huffed, and he puffed.

He huffed and he huffed

and he puffed and he puffed —

but he could NOT blow the brick house down.

The big bad wolf growled a big bad growl. He ran round the house, but the door was shut – tight, tight, tight. The windows were shut – tight, tight, tight. He looked at the roof, and he smiled.

"AHA!" said the big bad wolf, and up and up he climbed. He climbed into the chimney, and slid – wheeeeeeee! – all the way down, until he landed in the big pot of boiling water with an enormous

SPLASH!

"**YAROOOOOOOO!**" howled the wolf.
"**YAROOOOOOO!**"

He leapt out of the pot, back up the
chimney and onto the roof. Off he
jumped, and away he ran – away
and away and away . . . and
he never was seen again.

"Dear me," said the third little pig as she peeped into
the big pot. "That big bad wolf has quite spoiled our
parsnips and peppercorns. Never mind. We'll have green
pea soup instead."

And so they did . . .

OINK! OINK! OINK!

THE GINGERBREAD BOY

A long time ago, when stories were true, a little old woman and a little old man lived together in a little old house. They were happy enough, but sometimes they were lonely.

"I wish we had some company," said the little old woman.

"Someone to bring us a cup of tea," said the little old man.

The little old woman clapped her hands. "I know!

I'll make a little boy out of gingerbread. He shall have currant eyes, a smiley mouth, a cherry nose, and three shiny cherry buttons on his coat. I'll cook him in the oven until he is done – and he'll keep us company for ever and ever." And she went hurrying into her kitchen to weigh and mix and stir.

Quite soon there was a wonderful smell of hot gingerbread.

"When will our gingerbread boy be ready?" asked the little old man.

"He'll be ready when the clock strikes three," said the little old woman.

Sure enough, just as the clock struck three, there was a tap tap tapping from inside the oven.

"Let me out! Let me out!" called a voice.

The little old woman hurried to open the oven door, and the gingerbread boy jumped out.

"Welcome, gingerbread boy!" said the little old woman. "Welcome to our home!"

"And we'd like you to make us a nice cup of tea," said the little old man.

The gingerbread boy looked left, and the gingerbread boy looked right, and he frowned at the little old man.

"I've got three cherry buttons on my coat," he said. "I'm much too smart to do anything for anyone!

I'm as smart as smart can be –
I'm the gingerbread boy,
and you can't catch me!"

And he ran straight out of the open kitchen door and into the wide wide world outside.

The little old woman and the little old man went hurrying after him.

"Stop! Stop!" they called, but the gingerbread boy took no notice. Away and away he ran, over the green grassy field, and the little old woman and the little old man puffed behind him.

A black and white cow saw the gingerbread boy running by.

"Ooooh, little gingerbread boy," she mooed. "Come here and let me eat you!"

The gingerbread boy looked at the cow, and he pulled a face.

"Yah! Boo!" he shouted. "I've got three cherry buttons on my coat! I'm much too smart to be eaten by a cow!

I'm as smart as smart can be –

I'm the gingerbread boy, and you can't catch me!"

And he ran away from the cow and into the wood.

The black and white cow went trundling after him as fast as she could go.

"Stop! Stop! Come back and be eaten!" she mooed, but the gingerbread boy took no notice. Away and away he ran, in between the trees, and the black and white cow and the little old woman and the little old man puffed behind him.

A big brown horse saw the gingerbread boy running by.

"Hey, little gingerbread boy," he neighed. "Come here and let me eat you!"

The gingerbread boy looked at the horse, and he stuck out his tongue.

"Never! Never! Never!" he shouted. "I've got three cherry buttons on my coat! I'm much too smart to be eaten by a horse!

I'm as smart as smart can be –

I'm the gingerbread boy, and you can't catch me!"

And he ran away from the horse and along the river bank.

The big brown horse went galloping after him.

"Stop! Stop! Come back and be eaten!" he neighed, but the gingerbread boy took no notice. Away and away he ran, beside the rushing river, and the big brown horse and the black and white cow and the little old woman and the little old man puffed behind him.

A brown and whiskery fox saw the gingerbread boy running by.

"Good afternoon, young sir," said the fox. "My! What a hurry you're in!"

"I'm running away from a horse and a cow and a little old woman and a little old man!" said the gingerbread boy.

"I'm as smart as smart can be –
I'm the gingerbread boy, and they can't catch me!"

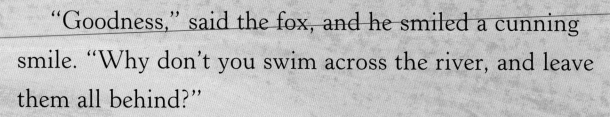

"Goodness," said the fox, and he smiled a cunning smile. "Why don't you swim across the river, and leave them all behind?"

The gingerbread boy stopped. He looked at the river. "I don't think I can swim," he said.

The fox shook his head. "Dear me, dear me," he said. "Maybe I could help? I'm just about to swim the river myself. You could ride on my tail!"

"Yes!" said the gingerbread boy. "Yes! I'll ride on your tail!"

So the gingerbread boy hopped onto the fox's tail.

The fox jumped into the river and began to swim.

He hadn't gone far when he said, "Gingerbread boy, you're too heavy for my tail. Climb up on my back!"

The gingerbread boy scrambled onto the fox's back, and the fox swam on. He swam and he swam, and then he said, "Gingerbread boy, you're too heavy for my back. Climb up on my nose!"

The gingerbread boy balanced himself on the fox's nose, and the fox swam on.

He swam and he swam and he swam, until he reached the bank on the other side of the river.

Then he licked his lips and he tossed the gingerbread boy up in the air – and he gobbled him ALL up.

CRUNCH! MUNCH!

YUM YUM YUM!

GOLDILOCKS AND
THE THREE BEARS

There was once a little girl called Goldilocks, and she did not always do as she was told. When one day her mother said, "You must NEVER EVER go into the woods on your own!" Goldilocks decided to do just that.

She waited until her mother was busy, and then

ran out of the door, singing, "La di da! La di dee!"

To begin with Goldilocks liked being in the woods.
Paths wound in and out of the trees, and Goldilocks
danced along first one and then another, until –

"Oh no!" she said. "I don't know where I am!"
She looked this way and that, but she didn't know
which way to go – and then she saw a curl of smoke
above the trees.

"A house!" Goldilocks said, and she ran and ran until she found herself standing in front of a little green gate. On the other side was a pretty pink cottage. Goldilocks hurried through the gate, and up to the blue front door.

Bang! Bang! Bang! She knocked as loudly as she could. Nobody answered, but the door swung open. Goldilocks crept inside.

She saw a saucepan bubbling gently on the stove, and a fire crackling and burning in the grate. A table was covered with a red spotty tablecloth. There were three chairs — a great big wooden chair, a middle-sized armchair, and a teeny tiny rocking chair with a bright red cushion. On the table were three bowls of porridge — a great big green bowl, a middle-sized pink bowl, and a teeny tiny red bowl.

Goldilocks licked her lips, and her tummy rumbled.

"I'm SO hungry," she said. She tiptoed up to the table, and took a spoonful of porridge from the great big bowl.

"YUCK!" said Goldilocks. "This porridge is much too salty!"

She took a spoonful from the middle-sized bowl.

"YUCK!" said Goldilocks. "This porridge is much too sweet!"

She took a spoonful from the teeny tiny bowl.

"YUM!" said Goldilocks. "This porridge is just right!" And she ate it all up, and licked the spoon.

"Ahhhh!" Goldilocks yawned. "I'm SO tired." And she went to sit in the great big chair.

"OUCH!" she said. "This chair is much too hard."

She hopped off the great big chair, and went to sit in the middle-sized chair.

"OOF!" said Goldilocks. "This chair's much too soft."

She scrambled out of the middle-sized chair, and squeezed herself into the teeny tiny chair.

"Ah!" said Goldilocks. "This chair's just right!" and she rocked herself to and fro and to and fro until –

CRASH!

The teeny tiny chair broke into seven different pieces.

"Bother," said Goldilocks, and she yawned a huge yawn. "Ahhhh! I'm SO sleepy. I think I'll have a little lie down." And she stumped up the stairs.

At the top of the stairs was a warm and cosy bedroom with red spotty curtains. All in a row were a great big bed, a middle-sized bed, and a teeny tiny bed.

"Just what I need," said Goldilocks, and she heaved herself into the great big bed.

"OUCH!" she said. "This bed is much too hard!"

She slid off the great big bed, and went to try the middle-sized bed.

"OOF!" said Goldilocks. "This bed's much too soft."

She slithered out of the middle-sized bed, and squashed herself into the teeny tiny bed.

"Ahhhh," she said, as she snuggled down. "This bed's just . . ." and she closed her eyes and fell fast asleep.

Outside the pretty pink cottage a great big Daddy Bear, a middle-sized Mummy Bear, and a teeny tiny Baby Bear were looking at the open front door.

"Someone's been into our house," said Daddy Bear in a great big voice.

"Someone's been looking inside," said Mummy Bear in a middle-sized voice.

"I want my porridge," said Baby Bear in a teeny tiny voice.

The three bears tiptoed into their house, and looked around.

"The saucepan's still bubbling," said Daddy Bear.

"The fire's still burning," said Mummy Bear.

"Look! Look! Look at the table!" said Baby Bear.

"Oh NO! Someone's been eating my porridge," said Daddy Bear.

"Someone's been eating my porridge," said Mummy Bear.

"Someone's been eating my porridge – and they've eaten it all up!" said Baby Bear.

Next they looked at their chairs.

"Oh NO! Someone's been sitting in my chair," said Daddy Bear.

"Someone's been sitting in my chair," said Mummy Bear.

"Someone's been sitting in my chair – and they've broken it all up!" said Baby Bear.

"Let's have a look upstairs," growled Daddy Bear, and the three bears climbed up the stairs to the bedroom.

"Oh NO! Someone's been sleeping in my bed," said Daddy Bear.

"Someone's been sleeping in my bed," said Mummy Bear.

"Someone's been sleeping in my bed," said Baby Bear,
"and – oh no! SHE'S STILL HERE!"
Daddy and Mummy Bear hurried to look, and
Goldilocks opened her eyes . . .

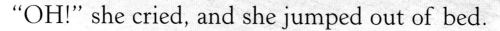

"OH!" she cried, and she jumped out of bed.

"BEARS!" she gasped, and she rushed down the stairs.

"MUM!" she shouted as she ran out of the cottage and down the path . . .

And she didn't stop running until she was safe at home with the front door shut behind her.

Daddy, Mummy and Baby Bear went down the stairs to the kitchen.

"Time for some porridge," said Daddy Bear in his great big voice, and he tied an apron round his great big waist.

"What about my chair?" asked Baby Bear in his teeny tiny voice.

"I'll mend it for you later," said Mummy Bear in her middle-sized voice.

And as Daddy Bear began to stir the saucepan of porridge, Baby Bear began to sing.

LA DI DA! LA DI DEE!

THE LITTLE RED HEN AND THE GRAIN OF WHEAT

Long long ago, a little red hen lived in a house with a dog and a cat and a duck. She was a busy little red hen, and she was always sweeping or cooking or sewing. The dog and the cat and the duck liked to watch her. They were far too lazy to do any work for themselves.

One day the little red hen found a grain of wheat. She went hurrying home with it, cluck cluck clucking in excitement as she bustled through the door.

"Look what I've found!" she said. "Who will help me plant it in our garden?"

"Not I," said the dog. "I'm MUCH too busy." And he ran round and round chasing a flea on his tail.

"Not I," said the cat. "I'm MUCH too busy." And she pranced out of the door to chase butterflies.

"Not I," said the duck. "I'm MUCH too busy." And he waddled off to swim in the pond.

"Then I'll do it myself," said the little red hen, and she did.

The little red hen planted the grain of wheat, and she watered it every day. She watched it grow from a small green shoot to a tall yellow stalk, and at last she saw that the ear of wheat was ripe.

"Look what a wonderful ear of wheat I've grown," she said. "Who will help me cut it?"

"Not I," said the dog. "I'm MUCH too busy." And he flopped down on the mat.

"Not I," said the cat. "I'm MUCH too busy." And she stretched herself out in a patch of sunshine.

"Not I," said the duck. "I'm MUCH too busy." And he shook the water off his back.

"Then I'll do it myself," said the little red hen, and she did.

The little red hen cut the ear of wheat, and dragged it onto a big smooth stone.

"This is a very fine ear of wheat," she said. "Who will help me thresh it?"

"Not I," said the dog. "I'm MUCH too busy." And he sat up to scratch his ears.

"Not I," said the cat. "I'm MUCH too busy." And she started to smooth her whiskers.

"Not I," said the duck. "I'm MUCH too busy." And he began to preen his feathers.

"Then I'll do it myself," said the little red hen, and she did.

When the little red hen had finished threshing she was left with a splendid heap of grain. "Look at that!" she said.

"Now, who will help me grind the wheat into flour?"

"Not I," said the dog. "I'm MUCH too busy." And he rolled on his back with his paws in the air.

"Not I," said the cat. "I'm MUCH too busy." And she began to lick her paws.

"Not I," said the duck. "I'm MUCH too busy." And he stood on one leg and winked at the cat.

"Then I'll do it myself," said the little red hen, and she did.

The little red hen was quite worn out after she had finished grinding the grain into soft white flour.

"Dear me," she said, "I'm SO tired. Won't one of you help me bake the flour into bread?"

"Not I," said the dog. "I'm MUCH too busy." And he closed his eyes and began to snore.

"Not I," said the cat. "I'm MUCH too busy." And she curled herself up in her basket.

"Not I," said the duck. "I'm MUCH too busy." And he tucked his head under his wing.

"Clucketty cluck," sighed the little red hen. "I'll do it myself."

The little red hen mixed the flour with yeast and water. She kneaded it and kneaded it until the dough was smooth. Then she popped it into a tin, and put it near the oven to rise.

"Woof?" said the dog, and he sniffed the air.

"Meeow?" said the cat, and she came to sit on the kitchen table.

"Quack?" said the duck, and he looked at the tin with his beady black eye.

The little red hen sat with her eyes tightly shut until the bread had risen. Then she got up and put the tin of dough in the very middle of the oven, and shut the oven door. It wasn't long until a delicious smell of crispy crusty bread filled the air.

"WOOF!" said the dog, and he wagged his tail.

"MEEOW!" said the cat, and she began to purr.

"QUACK!" said the duck, and he opened his beak wide.

The little red hen looked at the dog and the cat and the duck.

"Cluck," she said. "Now, who will help me eat this bread?"

"I will!" woofed the dog.

"I will!" purred the cat.

"I will!" quacked the duck.

"Oh no," said the little red hen, as she opened the oven and took out the delicious crispy crusty loaf. "I planted the grain of wheat. I cut the stalk. I threshed the grain. I ground the flour. I baked the bread. And now I shall eat it all up – me and my five little chicks!" And she opened the back door and called, "Cluck cluck cluck!" Her five little chicks came hurrying in . . . and they ate every crumb.

CLUCK CLUCK, CLUCKETTY CLUCK!

THE ENORMOUS TURNIP

Big Daddy George went out one day to sow some seeds.

"I'll help," said the little white mouse.

But Big Daddy George shook his head. "You're too little," he said. "Sowing seeds is a difficult job." And he sowed the seeds all by himself.

The sun shone, and the seeds grew – and so did the buttercups and daisies and dandelions.

"Time to do some weeding," said Big Daddy George.

"I'll help," said the little white mouse.

But Big Daddy George smiled a know-it-all smile. "No, no, my dear little mouse," he said. "Weeding is a hard thing to do. You just run away and play."

The seeds went on growing and growing, and Big Daddy George was pleased and proud.

"We'll soon have carrots and cabbages and cauliflowers," he said. "And beans and brussels and parsley and – Oh! My goodness gracious me! WHAT is that?" And Big Daddy George went hurrying down to the end of his garden.

"It's a turnip," said the little white mouse.

"So it is," said Big Daddy George, and he scratched his head. "It's a turnip. A big turnip. In fact, it's the biggest turnip I've ever seen. Well, well, well. Who'd have thought a turnip could grow so big?" And Big Daddy George went hurrying into his house to tell Old Granny Lola.

Every day from that day on Big Daddy George and Old Granny Lola came to stare at the turnip. They forgot about the carrots and cabbages and cauliflowers, and the beans and brussels and parsley. The little white mouse did his best, but it was hard to look after the garden all by himself. Besides, the parson and the doctor and the dentist and the schoolteacher and ALL the children from the school came to see the enormous turnip, and they trod here and stamped there, and squished and squashed the little green plants.

"Squeak," said the little white mouse, and helped himself to a pawful of parsley.

The turnip grew and grew and grew. It grew as big as the cat. It grew as big as the dog. It grew as big as the wheelbarrow. It grew as big as the cow. It grew as big as Big Daddy George . . .

"I think," said Big Daddy George, "it's time to pull our turnip up!"

"I'll help," said the little white mouse.

But Big Daddy George laughed and laughed and laughed. "YOU?" he said. "But this is an ENORMOUS turnip. You're MUCH too small, little white mouse."

And he strode down to the bottom of his garden, and grabbed the turnip firmly by its leaves, and he pulled and he pulled and he pulled . . . and the enormous turnip didn't move an inch.

"Come along, come along," said Old Granny Lola. "I'll help you." She took hold of Big Daddy George's braces and the two of them pulled and pulled and pulled . . .

and the enormous turnip didn't move an inch.

The parson, the doctor
and the dentist came hurrying
down the path.

"Here we are," they called.
"We'll have that turnip out of
the ground in a twinkling!"
And the parson grabbed hold
of Old Granny Lola's apron
strings. Then Big Daddy
George and Old Granny Lola
and the parson and the doctor
and the dentist pulled and
pulled and pulled . . .

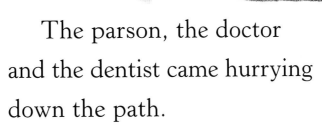

and the enormous turnip
didn't move an inch.

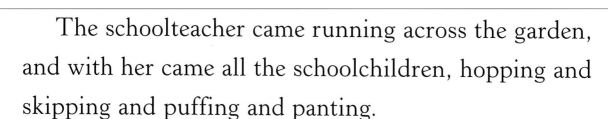

The schoolteacher came running across the garden, and with her came all the schoolchildren, hopping and skipping and puffing and panting.

"Wait for us!" they shouted. "We want to pull up the turnip!" And the teacher took hold of the dentist's coat tails. Then Big Daddy George and Old Granny Lola and the parson and the doctor and the dentist and the schoolteacher and ALL the children pulled and pulled and pulled . . .

and the enormous turnip didn't move an inch.

"Moo!" said the cow from the field next door, and she pushed her way through the hedge.

"Moo!" And she caught tight hold of the littlest girl's skipping rope. Then Big Daddy George and Old Granny Lola and the parson and the doctor and the dentist and the schoolteacher and ALL the children and the cow pulled and pulled and pulled. . . and the enormous turnip didn't move an inch.

"Woof!" barked the dog, and "Meeow!" mewed the cat, and they jumped up and caught hold of the cow's tasselled tail.

Then Big Daddy George and Old Granny Lola and the parson and the doctor and the dentist and the schoolteacher and ALL the children and the cow and the dog and the cat pulled and pulled and pulled . . . and the enormous turnip didn't move an inch.

The little white mouse hopped down from a flowerpot. "I'll help," he squeaked, and he clutched the cat's long furry tail. Then Big Daddy George and Old Granny Lola and the parson and the doctor and the dentist and the

schoolteacher and ALL the children and the cow and the dog and the cat and the little white mouse pulled and pulled and pulled and . . .

POP!

up came the enormous
turnip, and they all fell,
higgledy piggledy,
over and over.

"Thank you, little white mouse," said Big Daddy
George, as he picked himself up and dusted himself down.

"My pleasure," said the little white mouse, and that
evening he ate more turnip stew than anybody.

SQUEAK! SQUEAK! SQUEAK!

THE THREE WISHES

Far far away and long long ago, a woodcutter and his wife lived in a cottage under a tall old pine tree. Every day the woodcutter went into the forest to cut wood, and every day his wife waved him goodbye.

"Goodbye, Woodcutter!"

"Goodbye, Wife!"

"Be careful, Woodcutter!"

"I'll be careful, Wife!"

Every day the wife picked up her broom and swept the pine needles off the path. As soon as the path was neat and tidy she went back into her cottage, and made herself a cup of tea.

Every day she said to herself, "Mercy me. Sweeping pine needles makes me so tired. And I've still got the fire to light and dinner to cook!"

Then one cold and windy day, when there were more pine needles to sweep than usual, the woodcutter's wife had an idea. It was the first idea she had ever had, and she was very pleased with it. She waited all day at the gate for the woodcutter to come home from work.

"Woodcutter!" she said. "I've had an idea!"

The woodcutter shook his head. "Never a good thing, Wife. Tricksy things, ideas."

"But it's a good idea!" said the woodcutter's wife. "You must cut down the old pine tree!"

The woodcutter scratched his head. "Cut down the old pine tree, Wife? But why would I want to do that?"

His wife stamped her foot. "Don't you see, Woodcutter? If you cut down the old pine tree, there'll be no pine needles on the path! And if there are no pine needles, I won't have to sweep them away. And if I don't have to sweep them away, I won't get tired! Now, do as I say, or there'll be no dinner!"

"Yes, Wife," said the woodcutter.

"I'll do it straight away, Wife," and he picked up his axe and stepped towards the old pine tree.

He stopped in front of it, and bowed. "Excuse me, tree, but I must cut you down."

The pine tree shook from top to bottom. "Why must you do such a terrible thing?" it asked.

"My wife is tired of sweeping your pine needles from our path," said the woodcutter.

"But I don't want to be cut down," said the tree, and it waved its branches to and fro. "I'll tell you what. I'll give you three wishes if you promise to leave me alone."

The woodcutter rubbed his nose. Wishes were good things, he thought.

"Very well," he said. "I promise I won't cut you down. I'll take the three wishes, and go and have my dinner. I'm hungry!" And he hurried away with his axe over his shoulder.

The woodcutter walked into his cottage, and sat down at the table. He was surprised to see his wife cutting up bread and cheese.

"What!" he said. "No hot dinner?"

His wife shook her head. "When would I have had time to cook a hot dinner? I was waiting all day at the gate for you, Woodcutter. Now, have you cut the old pine tree down?"

The woodcutter was hungry, and being hungry made him cross.

"No," he said, "I haven't. It was a silly idea, and I want my dinner!"

His wife grew cross too. "It was NOT a silly idea!"

"It WAS! If you hadn't wasted your time having ideas, I'd be having a nice hot dinner! I wish I had a big fat meaty sausage!"

BOINGGGG!

The woodcutter's wife jumped, and the woodcutter stared and stared. There on the plate in front of him was a big fat meaty sausage.

"WHEREVER did that come from?" asked his wife, her eyes as big as saucers.

The woodcutter peered at the sizzling sausage. It smelt so good that his mouth began to water.

"It must be one of my wishes!" he said.

"Wishes? What wishes?" his wife asked.

"The pine tree gave me three wishes," the woodcutter told her.

"Mercy me!" said his wife. "You were given three wishes, and you wasted one on a sausage?"

The woodcutter shook his head. "I forgot about the wishes."

The woodcutter's wife jumped up from the table. "You forgot?" she shouted. "You forgot? Why, you could have wished for a brand-new house, and a horse and cart, and a heap of gold – but oh no! You wasted a wish on a sausage! How silly you are! Mercy me – I wish that sausage was stuck on your nose!"

BOINGGGG!

The big fat meaty sausage jumped off the plate and onto the woodcutter's nose.

The woodcutter jumped, and the woodcutter's wife stared and stared.

"Oh no no no! Whatever have I done?" she wailed, and she seized the sausage and she pulled and she pulled and she pulled . . . but the sausage stayed stuck.

"Ow! Ow! Ow!" yelled the woodcutter. "STOP! STOP! STOP!"

The woodcutter's wife sat back down in her chair with a FLOP!

"Oh, dear husband," she said, "whatever shall we do?"

The woodcutter sighed loudly. "There's only one thing to do," he said.

His wife sighed too. "Yes," she said.

And they held hands, and said together, "We wish the sausage was back on the plate!"

BOINGGGG!

And there was the big fat meaty sausage back on the plate. The woodcutter and his wife ate it for their dinner that night – and they both said it was the very best sausage they'd ever, ever eaten.

MERCY ME!

THE BILLY GOATS GRUFF

MAAAA! Little Billy Goat Gruff was hungry.
MAAAA! Middle-sized Billy Goat Gruff was very hungry.

MAAAA! Great Big Billy Goat Gruff was HUGELY hungry.

"There's nothing to eat in our field," said Little Billy Goat Gruff. "Not even a daisy."

"There's no green grass," said Middle-sized Billy Goat Gruff. "Not even a stalk!"

"There's nothing for breakfast or dinner or tea," said Great Big Billy Goat Gruff. "We've eaten it all up. We must go over the bridge and into the field on the other side of the stream."

Little Billy Goat Gruff looked up. "Oooh!" he said. "I can see buttercups and daisies!"

Middle-sized Billy Goat Gruff looked up too. "Oooh!" he said. "I can see fresh green grass!"

"I can see a field full of breakfasts and dinners and teas," said Great Big Billy Goat Gruff. "Little Billy Goat Gruff – you go first."

So Little Billy Goat Gruff skipped down the field and onto the bridge that crossed the stream.

Tippetty tappitty! Tippetty tappitty! went his four little feet on the old wooden bridge.

Tippetty tappitty! Tippetty –

"HOI! HOI! HOI!"

Up jumped a troll with a growl and a scowl. "Who's that tippetty tapping over my bridge?"

Little Billy Goat Gruff stood very still, but his knees trembled. "If you please, Mr Troll, it is I – Little Billy Goat Gruff!"

"A goat?" roared the troll, and his big eyes gleamed. "Yum yum yum! I'm going to eat you for my dinner, top to toe, tip to tail!"

"Oh, my little pointy hooves," said Little Billy Goat Gruff, and his voice was very small. "If you please, Mr Troll, I am only a very little billy goat. My brother is MUCH bigger than I am, and he's following right behind. He'll make a much better dinner for a big fierce troll like you."

"A BIGGER goat?" rumbled the troll, and he licked his lips. "Yum yum YUM! Be off with you – and don't come bothering me again!"

So Little Billy Goat Gruff hurried across the old wooden bridge – Tippetty tappitty! Tippetty tappitty! – into the field full of fresh green grass.

Middle-sized Billy Goat Gruff wasn't far behind.

He came trotting down the field and onto the bridge that crossed the stream.

Trip trap! Trip trap! went his four neat feet on the old wooden bridge. Trip trap! Trip –

"HOI! HOI! HOI!"

Up jumped the troll with a growl and a scowl. "Who's that trip trapping over my bridge?"

Middle-sized Billy Goat Gruff stood very still, but his knees knocked together. "If you please, Mr Troll, it is I – Middle-sized Billy Goat Gruff!"

"I've been waiting for you!" roared the troll. "Yum yum YUM! I'm going to eat you for my dinner, top to toe, tip to tail!"

"Oh, my pointed beard," said Middle-sized Billy Goat Gruff, and his voice shook. "If you please, Mr Troll, I am only a very middle-sized billy goat. My brother is MUCH bigger than I am, and he's following right behind. He'll make a much better dinner for a big fierce troll like you."

"A MUCH BIGGER goat?" rumbled the troll, and he rubbed his belly. "YUM YUM YUM! Be off with you – and don't come bothering me again!"

So Middle-sized Billy Goat Gruff hurried across the old wooden bridge – Trip trap! Trip trap! – into the field full of fresh green grass.

Great Big Billy Goat Gruff wasn't far behind.
He came marching down the field and onto the bridge
that crossed the stream.

TRAMP! TRAMP! TRAMP –

"HOI! HOI! HOI!"

Up jumped the troll with a growl and a scowl.
"Who's that tramping over my bridge?"

Great Big Billy Goat Gruff stood very still, but his
ears twitched. "It is I – Great Big Billy Goat Gruff!"
he said in his big gruff voice.

"I've been waiting for you!" roared the troll. "YUM YUM YUM! I'm going to eat you for my dinner, top to toe, tip to tail!"

"Oh, my great big pointed horns," said Great Big Billy Goat Gruff. "But, Mr Troll – I don't WANT to be eaten!"

And he rushed at the troll and
he caught the troll in his horns
and tossed him high in the air –
and the troll flew up and over
the end of the bridge, and fell
in the stream with a great big

SPLASH!

"And don't come bothering ME again!" snorted Great
Big Billy Goat Gruff, and he hurried across the old
wooden bridge – Tramp! Tramp! Tramp! – into the field
on the other side of the stream. And all three billy goats
ate buttercups and daisies and fresh green grass for their
breakfasts and dinners and teas until they were as fat
as butter, and as happy as the day is long.

Maaaa! MAAAA! **MAAAA!**

LITTLE RED RIDING HOOD

Little Red Riding Hood lived in a house at the edge of a wood full of tall green pine trees. Her father was a woodcutter, and every day he went out with his axe to chop up logs. Sometimes Little Red Riding Hood went with him and picked up sticks for firewood, and sometimes they went to see her grandmother, who lived in a cottage in the very middle of the wood. Sometimes she stayed at home with her mother, and helped her bake bread and cake and biscuits.

One day Little Red Riding Hood's mother called her into the kitchen.

"Dear Red Riding Hood," she said, "Grandma has a terrible cold, and I've packed her up a basket of bread and butter, and jam and cake. Do you think you could walk to her cottage on your own?"

Red Riding Hood nodded.

"Be very careful," said her mother. "And remember, whatever you do, keep to the path! And be sure to watch out for the big bad wolf."

Red Riding Hood nodded again. "I'll be careful," she promised, and she picked up the basket and went out of the house. Hoppitty skippetty! Hoppitty skippetty! Red Riding Hood skipped along the path, in between the tall trees. She hadn't gone far when she saw a patch of pretty yellow primroses . . . but they weren't by the path.

"They aren't very far away," Red Riding Hood said to herself, and she put her basket down. "I won't leave the path for long."

But as she hurried towards the flowers someone stepped out from behind a tree. Someone with a long nose. Someone with whiskers. Someone with a long furry tail.

"Good morning, little girl," said the someone, and he twirled his tail politely. "Shouldn't you be keeping to the path?"

Red Riding Hood stopped. "I'm only going to pick those primroses," she said. "My grandma's in bed with a terrible cold, and flowers will make her feel better."

"So they will," said the someone, and he helped Red Riding Hood pick a big bunch.

"That's a fine bunch of primroses," he said, "but now you should hurry along. Does your grandma live far from here?"

"She lives in the little pink cottage in the middle of the woods," said Red Riding Hood, and she picked up her basket.

"I see," said the someone, and he stroked his whiskers. "Now, be sure and keep to the path!"

"Oh, I will," said Red Riding Hood. "And thank you very much!"

"The pleasure," said the someone, "is mine." And he bowed before leaping away into the trees.

Red Riding Hood went on along the path with her flowers and the basket. She didn't see the someone hurrying as fast as he could go to her grandmother's cottage.

She didn't see the someone knocking at her grandmother's door, and jumping inside.

She didn't hear the someone howling, "Come out!" as her grandma slapped his paws and locked herself in a cupboard . . . and she didn't see the someone put on Grandma's best nightcap and nightie, and climb into Grandma's bed.

When Red Riding Hood reached her grandmother's cottage she opened the door and let herself in. The curtains were drawn, and it was dark inside. Red Riding Hood could just make out someone sitting up in bed with a nightcap on.

"Poor Grandma," said Red Riding Hood. "It's so dark I can't see you properly. Are you feeling very bad?"

There was a loud cough, "Ahem ahem AHEM!"

Then a terrible sneeze, "Atchoo atchoo ATCHOO!"

and Red Riding Hood stepped closer. She rubbed her eyes, and looked again.

"Grandma!" she said. "What big ears you have today!"

"All the better to hear you with, my dear," said a growly voice.

Red Riding Hood stepped a little closer.

"Oh, Grandma!" she said. "What big eyes you have today!"

"All the better to see you with, my dear," said the growly voice.

Red Riding Hood stepped closer still.

"Grandma!" she said. "What big teeth you have today!"

"All the better to EAT you with, my dear!" said the growly voice, and the wolf threw off the nightcap and tried to jump out of the bed –

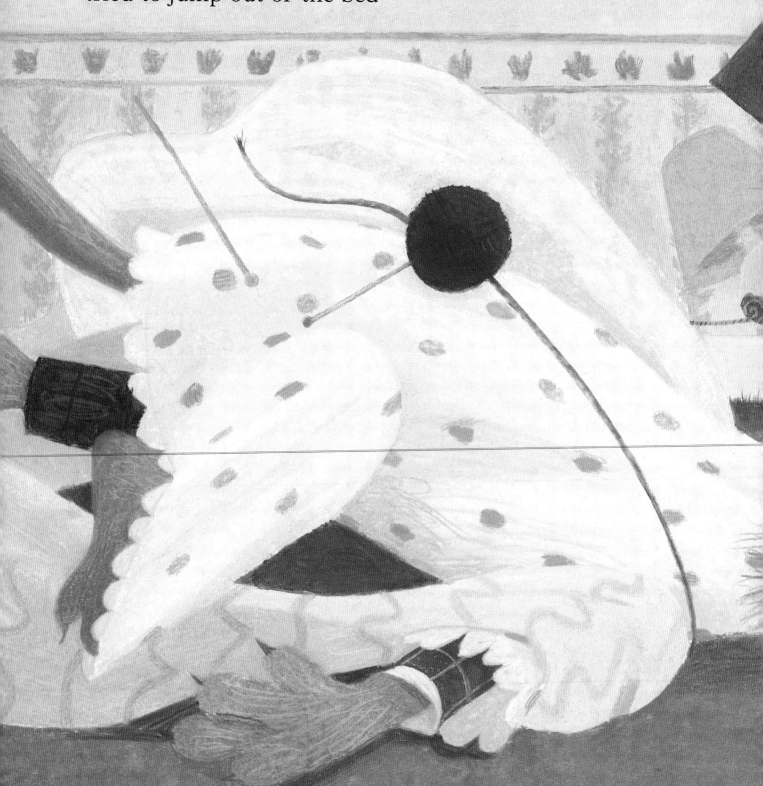

but he tangled his toes in
Grandma's nightie and
he fell on the floor –

CRASH!

And just as Grandma threw open her cupboard, Red
Riding Hood's father strode in through the door.

"YAROOO!" howled the wolf,
and he jumped out of the window,
and went hopping and limping
down the path . . . and that was
the last that anyone saw of him.

"I think," said Grandma, "that it must be time for tea!"
And she unpacked the basket that Red Riding Hood had
brought her, and they all ate bread and butter, and jam
and cake – and very delicious it was too. Then Red Riding
Hood and her father washed the dishes, kissed Grandma
goodbye, and went happily home together.

HOPPITTY! SKIPPETTY! HOPPITTY HOP!

THE END